When I grow up

A story from Mali

Written by Cyprien K.M. Akuete
Illustrations by Karim Diallo

(in collaboration with CEBA)

NAE

They tell me that, when I was
young, I was very small.
In fact, they say that I was really tiny.

They said I could even fit
into a box like this one.

Then I started growing and I got a little bigger. But I could still fit into a big suitcase like this one.

They said that I would grow some more and that, one day, I would be bigger than the suitcase...

... and bigger
than this bookcase.

I will be able to pick a ripe mango
from the tree in the garden,
just by stretching out my arms.

I will help Mama with the washing
and I will be able to hang the clothes
on the washing line by myself.

I will be able to put away
the hoe after working with
Papa on the farm.

Oh, I wish I was a grown up!
"Mama, when will I be big?"

"Papa, make me grow faster!
I want to get big quickly!"

I want to be a grown up.
I want to work hard, very hard,
to feed all the children.

Then the world will be a better place.
No one will be hungry or afraid.

I want to be a lawyer so that I can
use the law to help people.

First published 2001
Second Impression 2008
Africa Christian Press
P.O. Box AH 30, Achimota
Ghana
Tel: +233 21 244147/8
Fax: +233 21 220271
E-mail: acpbooks@ghana.com

and

New Africa Books (Pty) Ltd
99 Garfield Road
Claremont 7700
South Africa

New Africa Education (NAE) is an imprint of New Africa Books (Pty) Ltd

Originally published in French as *Quand je serai grand*
© Le figuier/EDICEF 1999

© Africa Christian Press

ISBN 10: 1-919876-11-1
ISBN13: 978-1-919876-11-5

Translation and adaption from French: Data & Decisions Consulting
Editor: Richard A.B. Crabbe
Proofreading: Fiona Macgregor
Typesetting: Jenny Wheeldon

Printed and bound in the Republic of South Africa by Pinetown Printers